I Want a Horse

By Mikaela Vincent

To my daughter,
who rides
with me
and shares
my dreams...

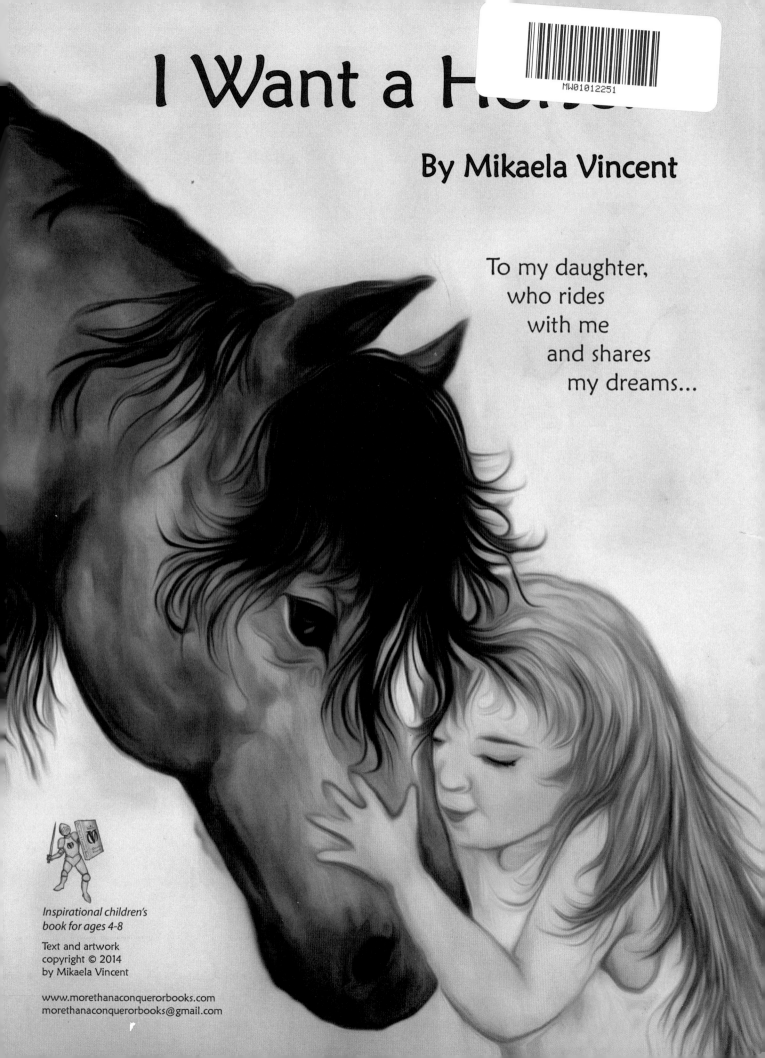

Inspirational children's book for ages 4-8

"I want a horse,"
    dear Kimberly said.

"A horse of my own
    to sleep next to my bed."

"He could be my best friend and join me for tea."

"We could play hide and seek.
I think he'd like me."

"That's nice," said Mom.
"But your room is too small.
What a horse really needs
is a field and a stall."

"But I want a horse that belongs to just me.
If I had a horse, how happy I'd be!

I could ride anytime,
    anyplace, anywhere.
I could feed him and pet him
    and brush his soft hair.

On warm, sunny days
    we could go for a walk.
We could ride to the park,
    have a picnic and talk."

"We could gallop so fast,
his mane whips my face.
My horse and I,
we'd win every race."

"That's nice," said Mom.
"But we live in the city.
A horse is too big.

. . . How about a kitty?"

"I can't ride a cat! That idea's insane.
I'd squash it and cause it
a whole lot of pain!

Besides, kitties scratch
and mess up the place.

They leap from high places . . .

. . . and land in your face!"

"A horse would be better,
so mighty and strong.
My own horse and I,
we'd sure get along."

"That's nice," said Mom.
"But it can't
come up here.
We live on the
twenty-third
floor, my dear."

"We could walk up the stairs one flight at a time.
I think I could do it, 'though it'd be quite a climb."

"But a horse needs a place to gallop and play.
You can't keep it here. There just is no way.
It wouldn't be fair to the horse, dearest Kim.
You're just thinking of you.
You're not thinking of him.
A horse like that is not what you need.
Such a great horse would be hard to feed.
Not to mention manure, pile upon pile.
You could hardly clean that up with a smile!"

"Maybe you're right.
Moms always are.
Maybe you'd rather
me ask for a . . ."

"Kimberly, dear,
      you've said quite enough.
            There's much more to life
                  than just wanting stuff."

                              "I'm sorry, Mom," sad Kimberly said.
                                    "But the dream of a horse
                                          is just stuck in my head."

Mom saw the tear in Kimberly's eye.
      She hugged her and kissed her
            and said with a sigh,

"Not so long ago, I was like you.
      I wanted a horse of my very own too."

"The horse of my dreams
    was a dapple grey
with silver wings
    to carry me away."

"At night she would come
to my room and we'd fly
over houses and valleys
and mountains so high."

"We'd soar over India . . .

. . . Austria,

. . . and Maine.

She knew where to go.
I needed no rein."

"Sometimes we'd light on a mountain of snow,
or sit by a lake in the bright moon's glow."

"Moms dream of horses?" Kim gasped with surprise.
"But you're all grown up! Is dreaming so wise?"

"Yes, I dreamed of horses, just as you do.
     I still dream sometimes. It's all right for me to.
I think when God made me, He already knew
     That I'd have a daughter who loves horses too.
I may be grownup, but deep down inside,
     a piece of my heart still longs to ride,
to feel the wind whip and lash at my hair,
     as I dash over hills on a painted mare.
Kimberly dear, we both are blessed,
     for dreams of horses are some of the best!"

Kimberly laughed. "Our horses should meet,
     your dream and mine. Now that would be sweet!"

"I'd like that," Mom said.
   "Our horses could prance
in the sea and the sand
     on the south side of France."

"We could visit the king
of some far-off place.
We could bow at his throne
with courtly grace."

"We could dance on a cloud, eat a piece of the sky,
put stars in our hair, see the earth from up high.

"Dreaming with you
    is a fun thing to do!"

"Oh, Mom," said Kim,
    "I sure love you!

I'd still like a horse,
    but I guess
        that you're right.
Fitting a horse
    in my room
        would be tight.

I don't want smelly piles
    all over my floor.

        I don't want to haul hay . . ."

"I like **this** more!"

Maybe one day my dream
 will come true.
But what I like best

 is **being with You.**

I guess I'll enjoy
 what's already mine,
and save my own horse
 for some other time."

My horse I dream of

Pure-As-Gold Children's Books
Equipping young hearts today
for the battles of tomorrow.

by Mikaela Vincent

I Want a Horse!
Draw My Own Storybook
By Mikaela Vincent

If you could have any horse, what would your horse be like? Where would you go together? What would you do?

Dream big with the story starters on the wide-open pages of this color-pencil drawing book for kids based on author Mikaela Vincent's *I Want a Horse!*

For horse lovers journals, middle school fantasy novels, and other good books for children, teens, tweens, youth, parents, homeschool, leaders, and families, visit

www.MoreThanAConquerorBooks.com.

We're not just about books. We're about books that make a difference in the lives of those you care about.

Step into the adventure...

Mikaela Vincent
More Than A Conqueror Books

We're not just about books. We're about books that make a difference in the lives of those you care about.

www.MoreThanAConquerorBooks.com

www.morethanaconquerorbooks.wordpress.com
morethanaconquerorbooks@gmail.com